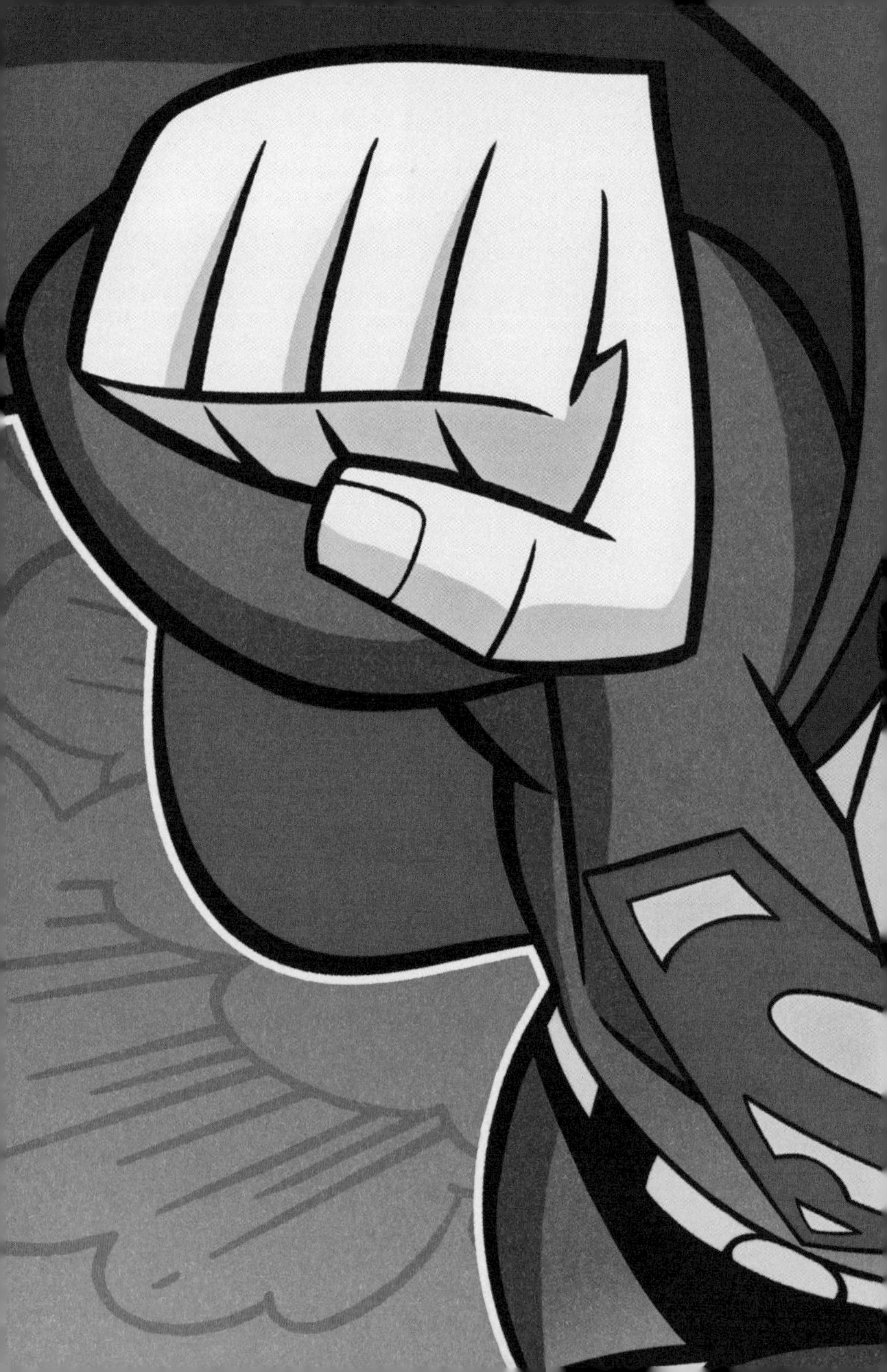

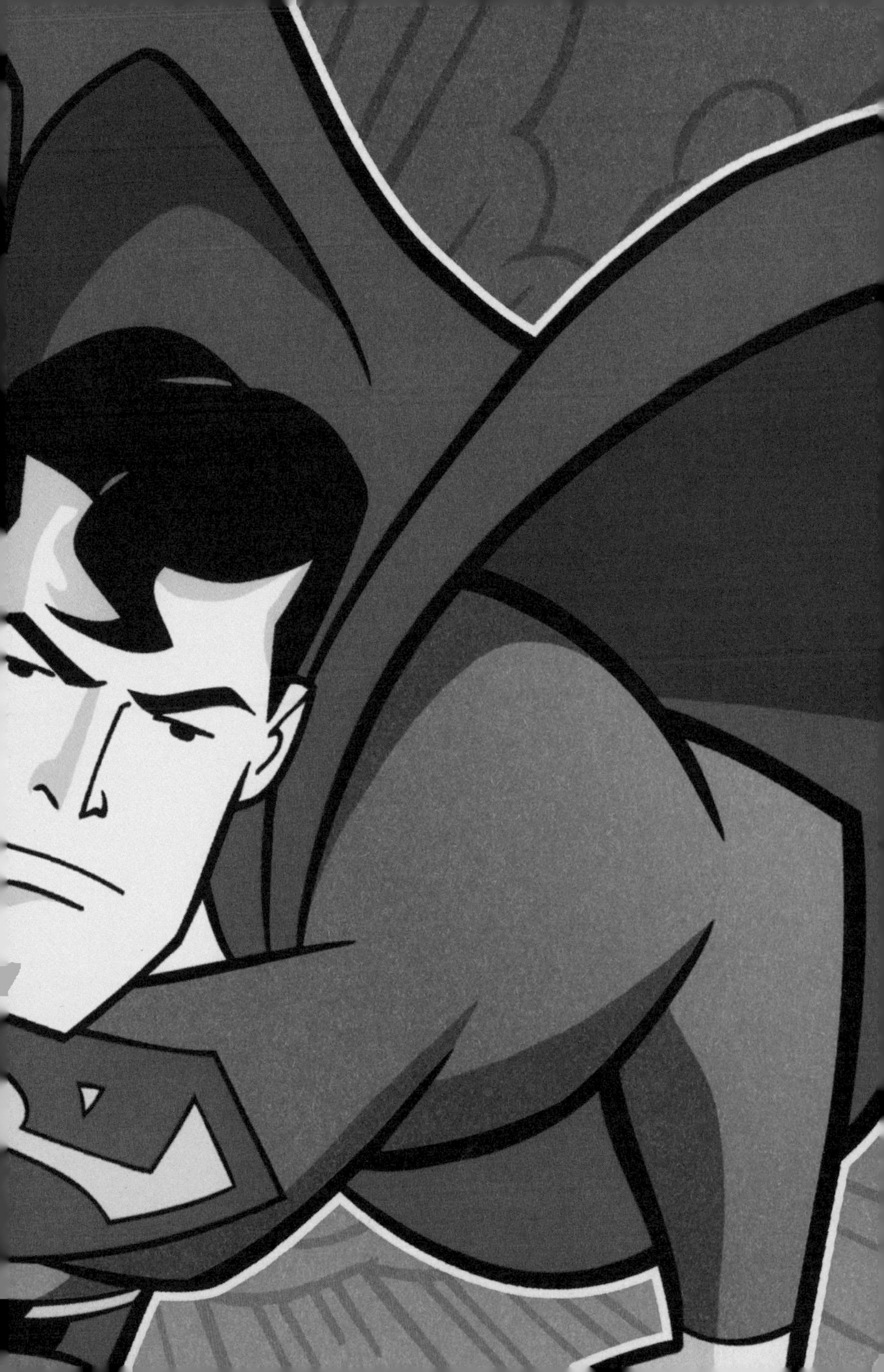

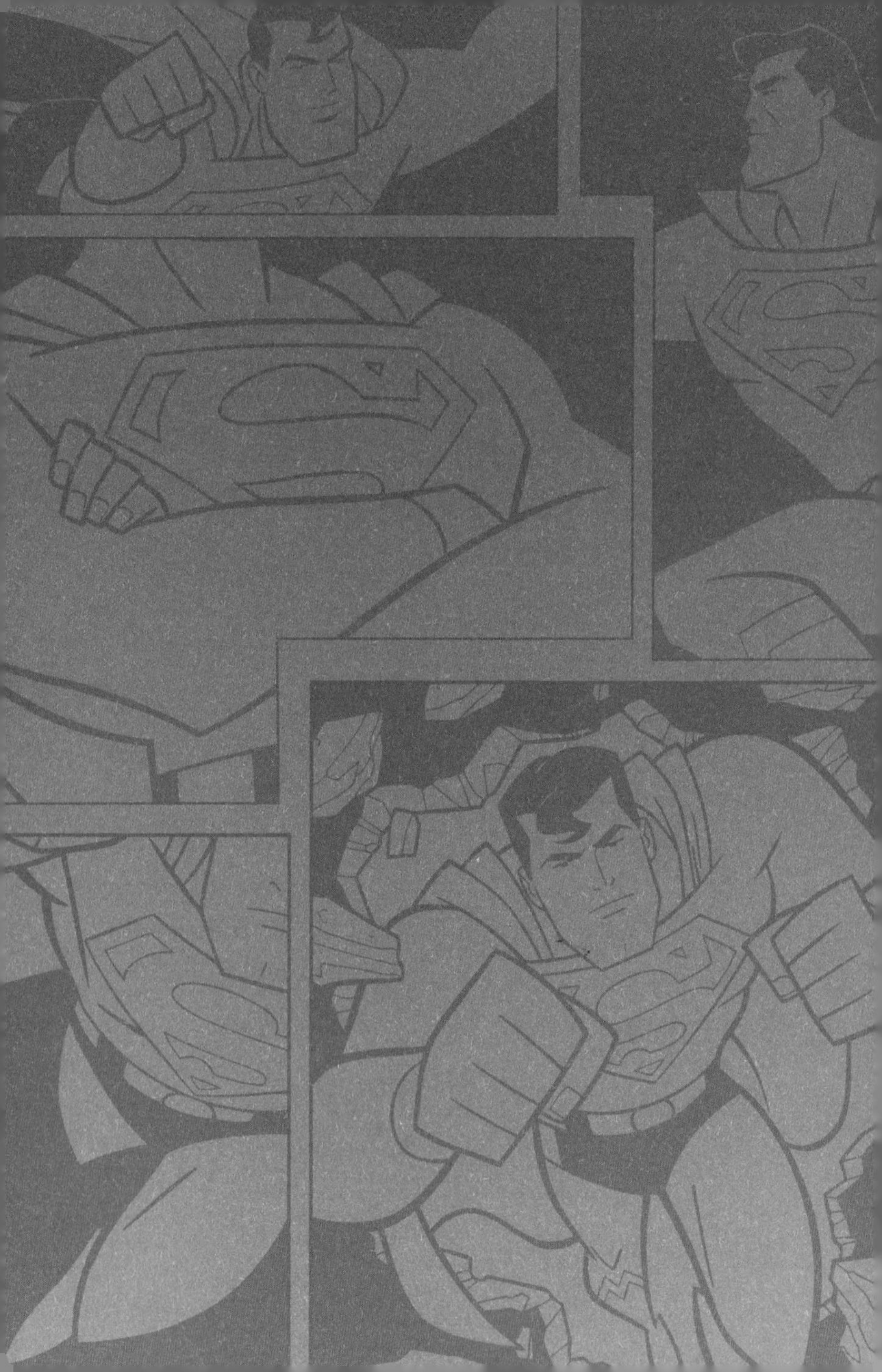

HEROES

SUPERMAN

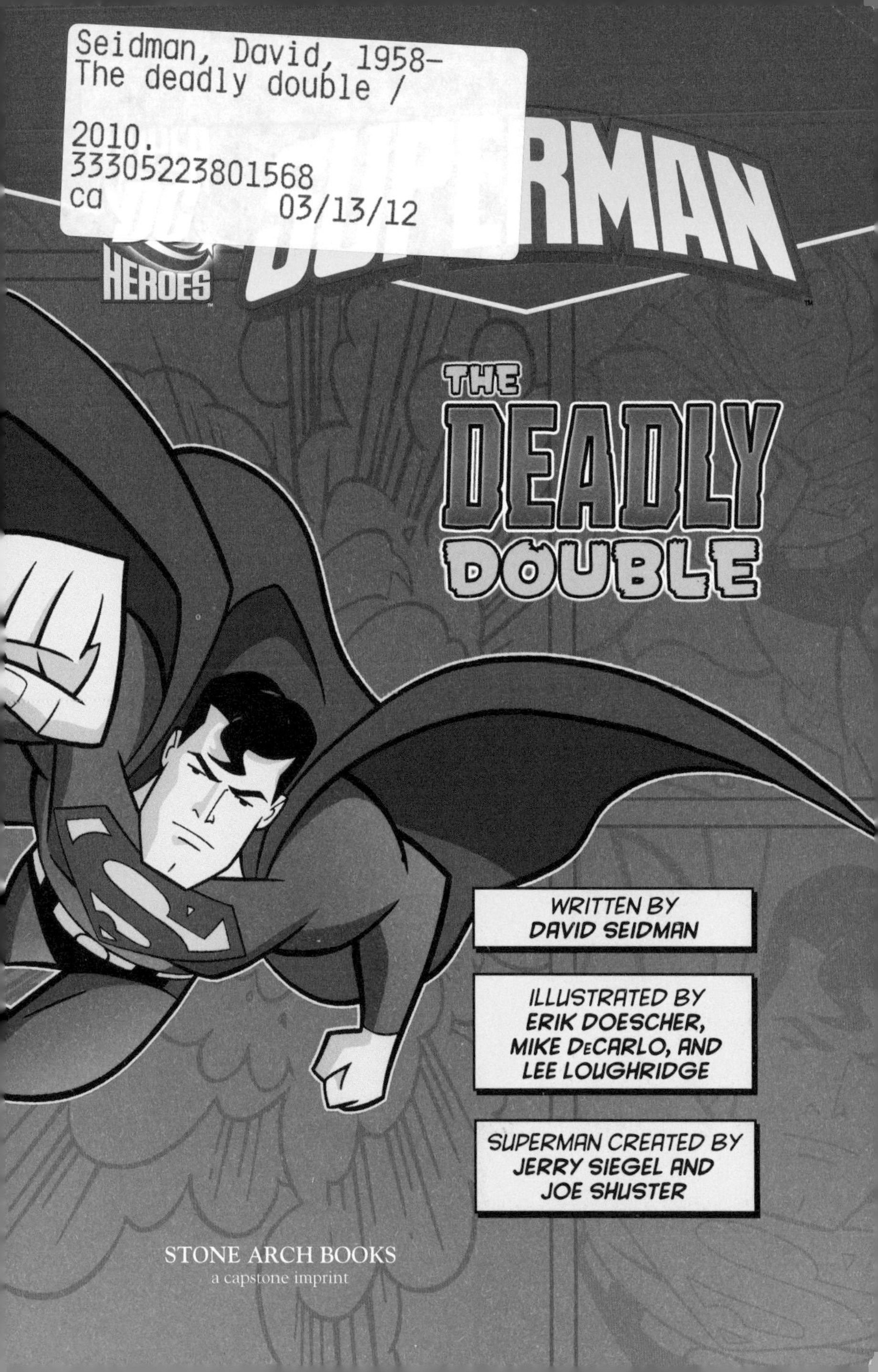

THE DEADLY DOUBLE

WRITTEN BY
DAVID SEIDMAN

ILLUSTRATED BY
ERIK DOESCHER,
MIKE DeCARLO, AND
LEE LOUGHRIDGE

SUPERMAN CREATED BY
JERRY SIEGEL AND
JOE SHUSTER

STONE ARCH BOOKS
a capstone imprint

Published by Stone Arch Books in 2010
A Capstone Imprint
151 Good Counsel Drive, P.O. Box 669
Mankato, Minnesota 56002
www.capstonepub.com

Library of Congress Cataloging-in-Publication Data

Seidman, David, 1958-
  The deadly double / by David Seidman ; illustrated by Erik Doescher ;
illustrated by Lee Loughridge ; illustrated by Mike DeCarlo.
    p. cm. -- (DC super heroes. Superman)
  ISBN 978-1-4342-1571-0 (library binding) -- ISBN 978-1-4342-1726-4
(pbk.)
  [1. Superheroes--Fiction.] I. Doescher, Erik, ill. II. Loughridge, Lee, ill.
III. De Carlo, Mike, ill. IV. Title.

PZ7.S45542De 2010
[Fic]--dc22   2009029095

Summary: After chasing the evil Mala through space, Superman returns
to Earth, and he finds people running from him. While Mala had decoyed
Superman, her partner, Jax-Ur, disguised himself as Superman and
terrorized the world. Now Jax-Ur and Mala plan to save the people of
Earth from Superman, become their new hero, and lead them in Jax-Ur's
quest to take over the planet. Superman has to stop Jax-Ur and Mala, but
it's not easy when they have the whole world on their side.

Art Director: Bob Lentz
Designer: Hilary Wacholz
Production Specialist: Michelle Biedscheid

Printed in the United States of America
092009
005619WZS10

TABLE OF CONTENTS

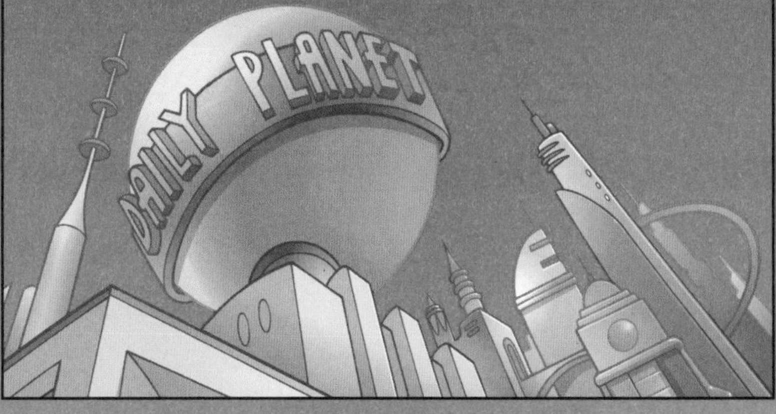

DAILY PLANET

CHAPTER 1

WILD WARRIOR WOMAN

Superman sped past stars and planets and asteroids. He was in hot pursuit of a warrior woman named Mala.

Mala, like Superman, was born on the planet Krypton. Both of them had amazing superpowers. Kryptonians could hear and see more sharply than any human. They could also fly at super-speed, shrug off bullets, and lift entire mountains.

Superman used his powers to help people. Mala, however, simply wanted to make them her slaves.

On Krypton, she had helped a general named Jax-Ur try to take over the planet. Krypton's leaders had punished them both by putting them into the Phantom Zone, a universe of pain and loneliness.

Now, Mala was free, and she was angry. Superman had to catch her before she caused any real damage to Earth.

He reached for her booted foot, but he couldn't grab hold of it. Mala was flying as fast as Superman himself. She remained just a few inches beyond his reach.

Mala glanced over her shoulder as her visor slid up. A big smirk came to her lips.

BZZT! Two razor-thin lines of heat vision shot from her eyes. The red-hot beams were headed right for Superman's space suit.

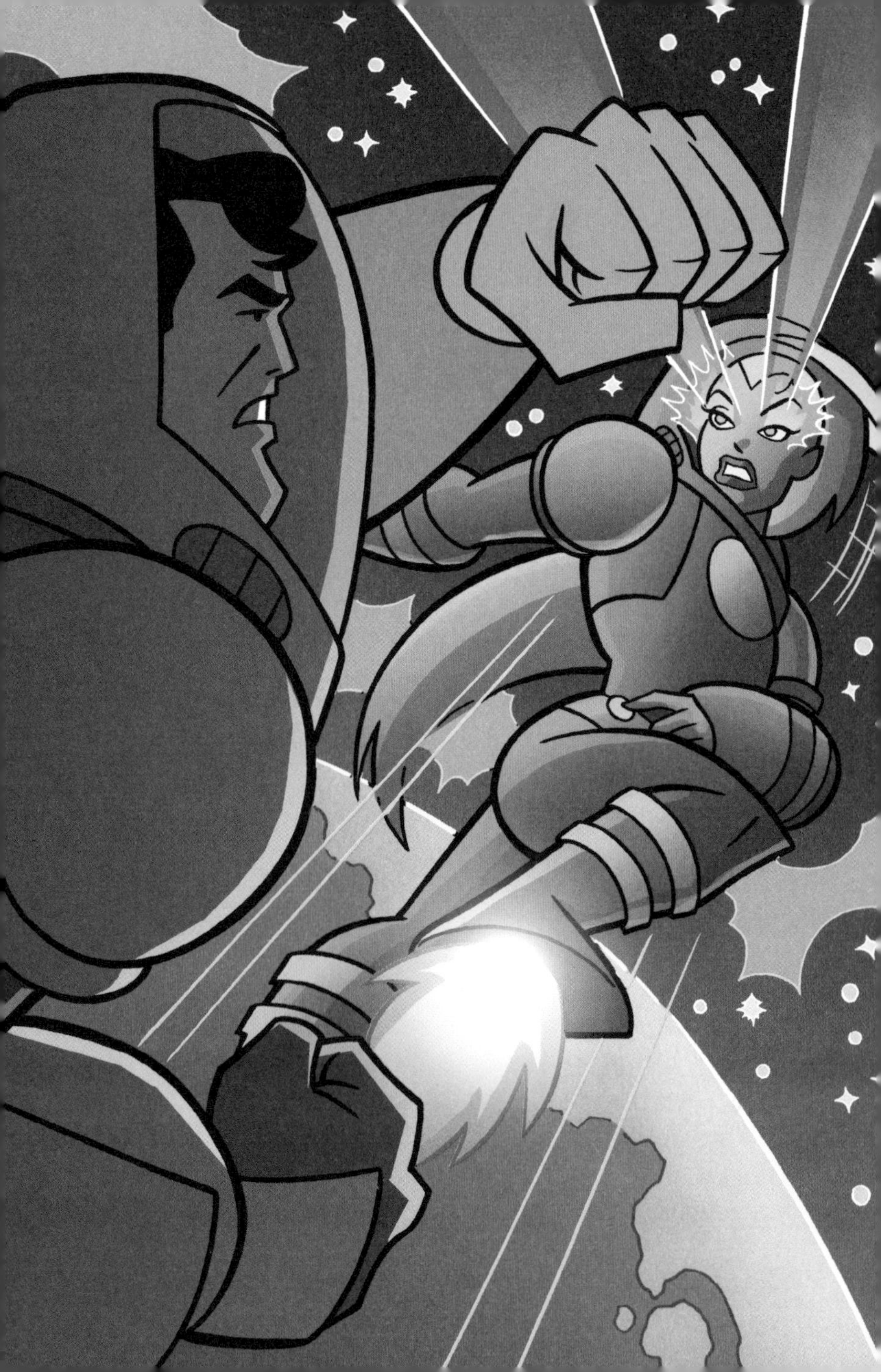

Superman jerked out of the beams' path, narrowly avoiding the blast. Then Mala sped away from him once again.

Superman could tell Mala was toying with him, but he didn't know why. Mala wasn't the type of person to hit and run. She preferred to attack head-on.

Superman first met Mala years ago when he had mistakenly freed her from the Phantom Zone. Mala had then freed Jax-Ur, and they'd tried to conquer Earth. But with the help of friends like the gutsy reporter Lois Lane, Superman had sent them back to the Phantom Zone.

WHAM! Something bulky slammed into Superman. Mala had just zoomed past.

She's heading back toward Earth! Superman thought.

Superman quickly turned to chase her. He couldn't figure out why Mala was returning to Earth after leading him into space. Of course, that was only one of the things he wanted to know.

Superman had last seen Jax-Ur and Mala when they had escaped from the Phantom Zone and taken over an alien world. Superman had raced to the planet and fought them. During the fight, they had tried to throw Superman into a black hole. But instead, Jax-Ur and Mala had fallen into the black hole themselves.

How did they get out? Superman wondered. *Maybe they found —*

Suddenly, a thousand rocks rammed into Superman. Through the storm of stone, he could see Mala throwing asteroids toward him at super-speed.

CRUNCH! Superman smashed through the rocks as he flew toward Mala. His body ached. He had been chasing Mala for a long time.

Hours earlier, Superman had been walking through downtown Metropolis. He was heading to work as *Daily Planet* newspaper reporter Clark Kent. Suddenly, Mala had flown to the center of town. She yelled, "Kal-El of Krypton, also known as Superman! I have come to destroy you. Face me, you coward!"

Clark had quickly changed into Superman. He flew toward Mala, but she rocketed into space. He'd been chasing her around the solar system ever since.

Superman strained to gain some speed. Suddenly, an asteroid screamed toward him.

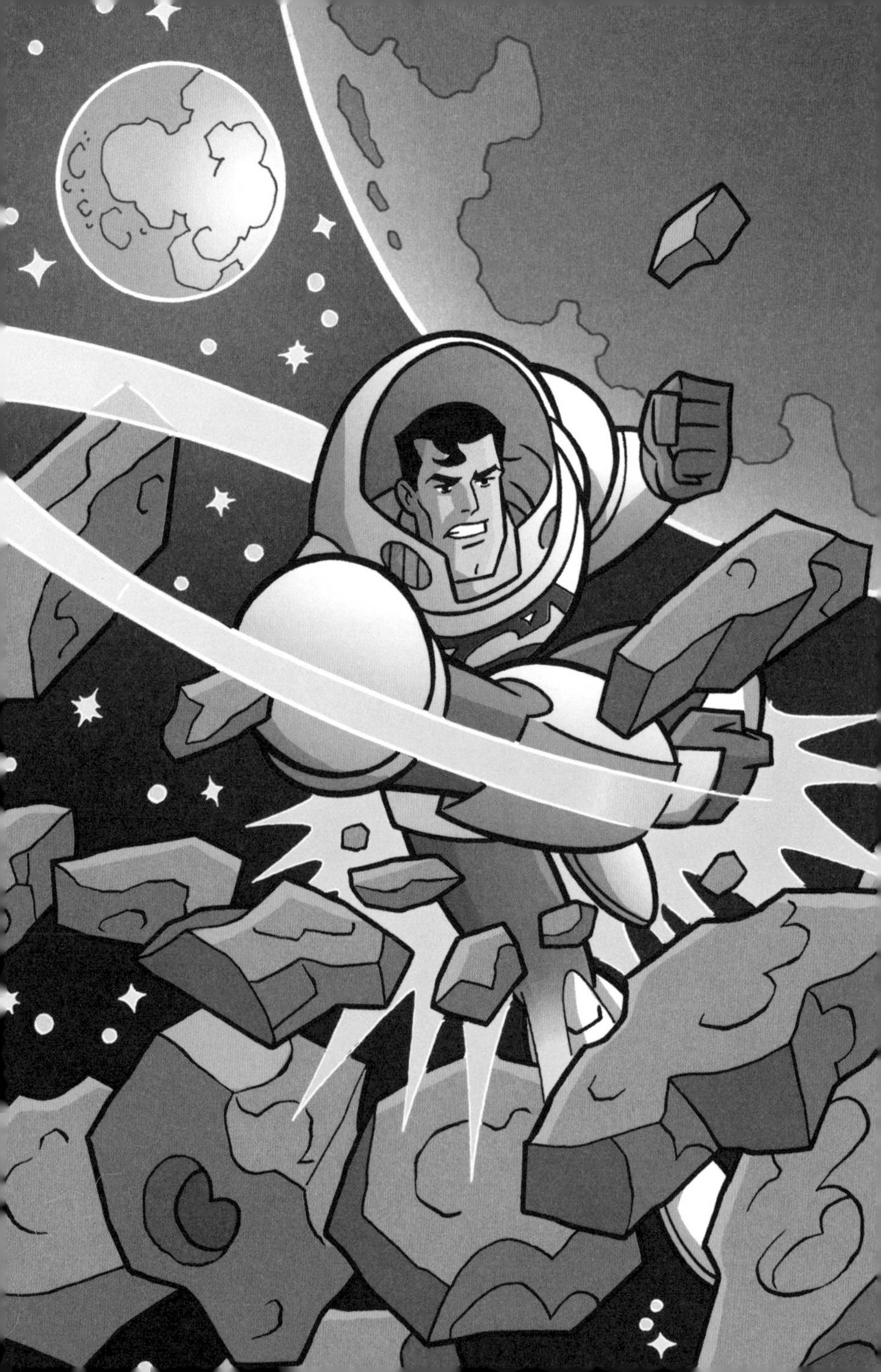

SMASH! The debris from the impact flew everywhere. Dust swirled around him, but with his X-ray vision, Superman could still see. Mala was heading toward Earth, but slowing down long enough to gather and throw more asteroids at him.

Superman bolted toward Mala and grabbed her wrists. The two super-beings wrestled and punched each other.

As they tumbled through space, Superman noticed that Mala was pushing him toward Earth.

When he caught sight of the planet, Superman gasped in surprise. Famous places no longer looked the way they used to. Streets in Metropolis had been ripped up. Mountains in Asia were piles of rock. Lakes had dried up. Forests were shattered into splinters.

Just then, Mala landed a punch that sent Superman plunging toward Earth. She smiled and flew after him. Just before she reached him, Superman saw who was destroying his planet. He stared at the man in sick shock.

He looked just like Superman himself!

CHAPTER 2

THE SECOND SUPERMAN

WHAM! Mala slammed into Superman's belly and pushed him downward. As he fell, Superman grabbed Mala's arms and hurled her back into space. He quickly looked for the fake "Superman" who was attacking his world. In the distance, he saw the impostor shred a Vermont forest into rows of splinters.

With his super-vision, Superman took a closer look. As he suspected, "Superman" was actually Jax-Ur wearing a Superman disguise.

POW! SLAM! A flurry of punches and kicks assaulted Superman. Mala was back, howling with warrior rage. She grabbed Superman by the arm and threw him into the same forest that the fake "Superman" was destroying.

KRASSSHHH! Trees fell into the crater that the impact of Superman's body had made, but he shrugged them off like toothpicks. He saw Jax-Ur turn toward the sound of the crash. "Superman" smiled and flew at super-speed into a hillside cave.

He emerged as Jax-Ur, a giant of a man. He had a black goatee and wore a high-tech eye patch. He launched out of the cave like a rocket.

Mala raked her sharp fingernails down Superman's chest. It hurt, but Superman was more concerned with a whirring noise.

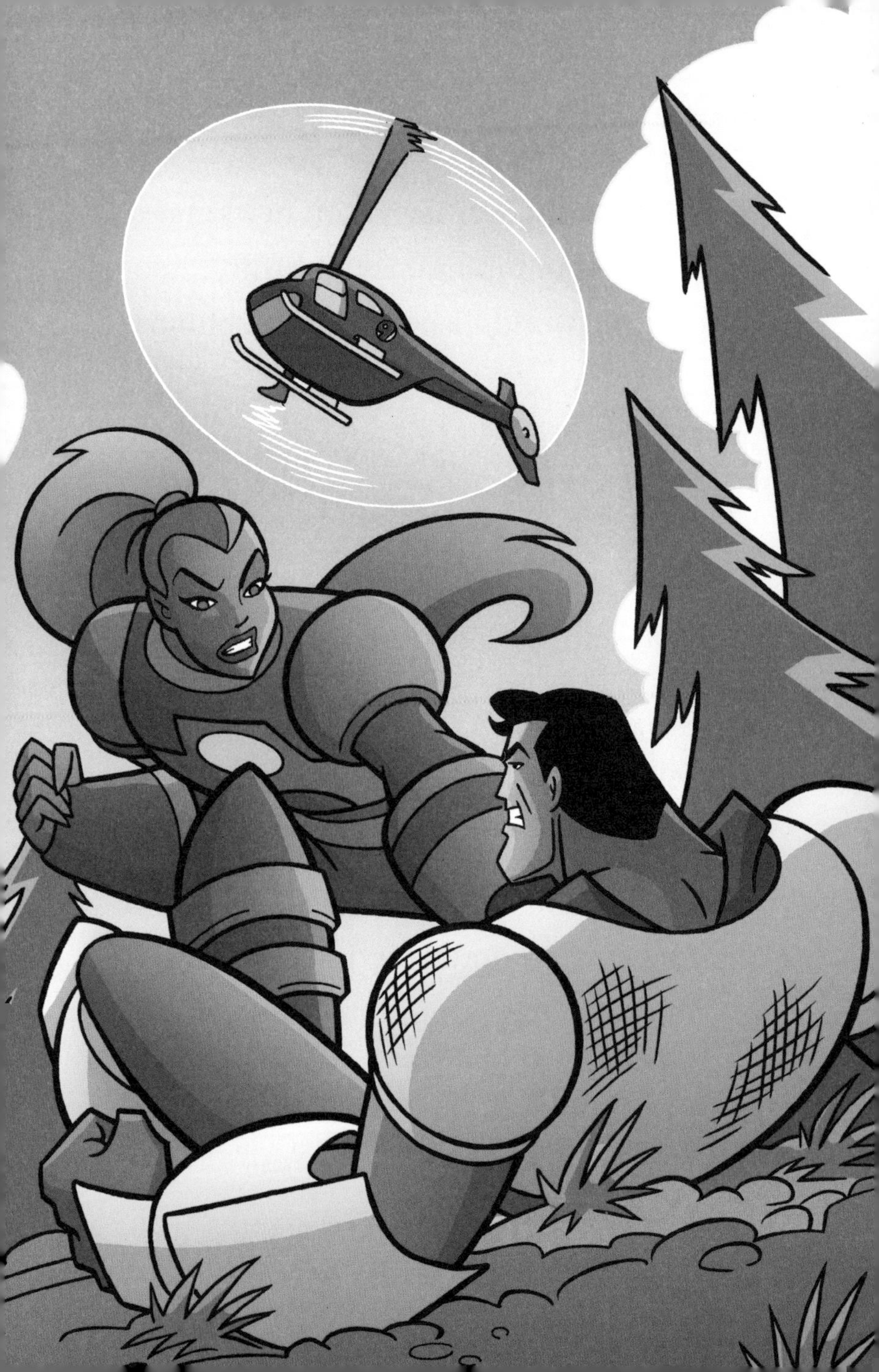

It was the **WHIR-WHIR-WHIR-WHIR!**
of helicopter blades. Television news crews were in the air, taping his fight with Mala. All over the world, people were watching.

Superman could hear them talk about the battle. Many people were confused by the charade.

"I can't believe my eyes!" a hairdresser in Tokyo said. "It looked like Superman was attacking us!"

"What's going on?" murmured a nurse in Argentina. "Superman has always protected our planet before."

Mala snarled and reared back to send a punch toward Superman's mouth.

THUD! He caught her fist before it could land, and swung her over his head and onto the ground.

KRAK! She smashed onto her back with amazing force. He leaned in toward her ear as his hands pressed her into the dirt. "You've been beating me because I've been busy trying to figure out what's going on," Superman said, "but I'm not going to do that anymore. You're going to tell me what I need to know."

Then, suddenly, Superman felt like a truck hit him. He tumbled along the forest floor until he hit the base of a mountain. He hurt all over, from the scratches on his face to the bruises on his belly. He looked up at what had hit him.

It was Jax-Ur. With his fists on his hips, the general stood tall and straight and bold. "You might beat Mala," he said in a smooth, deep voice, "but you can't beat me!"

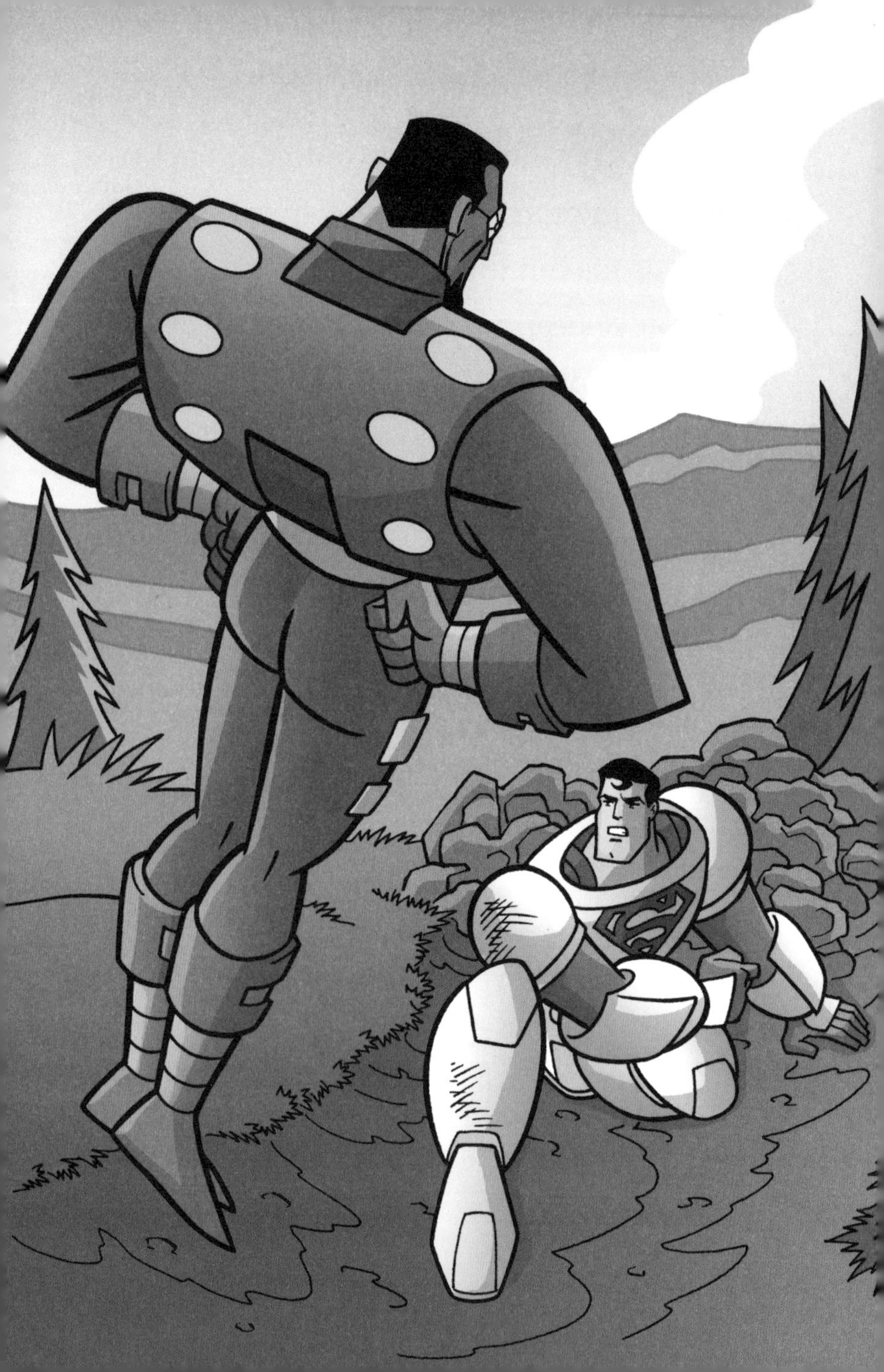

Mala rose into the sky and hovered next to Jax-Ur. "Even if you could beat Jax-Ur, you surely couldn't beat both of us," Mala said. She looked almost as badly hurt as Superman, but her grin told him that she was ready for more fighting.

ZZZRRRRTT! Jax-Ur and Mala fired beams of heat-vision at Superman. Quickly, the Man of Steel gripped the ground and hurled globs of dirt into their faces. For a moment, they coughed and batted the dirt away.

Superman used the moment to escape. He tunneled into the ground at super-speed, away from the other Kryptonians.

"Get him!" he heard Jax-Ur command. Like a dog digging for a bone, Superman started whipping handfuls of dirt and rocks behind him.

As Superman tunneled, he scanned the dirt around him. With his X-ray vision, he could see through most of the underground world, but one area a few miles away blocked his sight. He shifted his course and headed in its direction.

"I see him!" Mala shouted as Superman turned. *BZZT!* She fired her heat vision at him. The beams carved holes in the underground rock. Suddenly, to Mala's surprise, Superman darted behind something that she couldn't see through.

Mala and Jax-Ur dug to the spot that blocked their vision powers. It was a thick slab of lead ore.

"Of course," Jax-Ur said. "Our X-ray vision can't see through lead." They pounded through the soft metal only to find that Superman had disappeared.

There was no way to catch him now. In the dirt beyond the lead wall, Superman had cut several tunnels. Jax-Ur and Mala didn't know which tunnel to follow. Mala gritted her teeth and growled.

"Calm down, Mala," Jax-Ur said in a soothing tone. "I've planned for a problem like this. I have Superman right where I want him." He smiled. "Let's go. In a few minutes, the whole world will be helping us."

CHAPTER 3

ESCAPES AND EVIL

While Jax-Ur and Mala were pounding through the wall of lead, Superman was flying to Metropolis. *I have to find out what's going on,* he thought. *And the best place to do that is my newspaper.*

He landed on the Daily Planet's rooftop. In the blink of an eye, he changed into his Clark Kent clothes and glasses, and sped downstairs.

Clark stepped inside the Daily Planet newsroom. Immediately, he heard a voice ask, "Clark! Where have you been all day?"

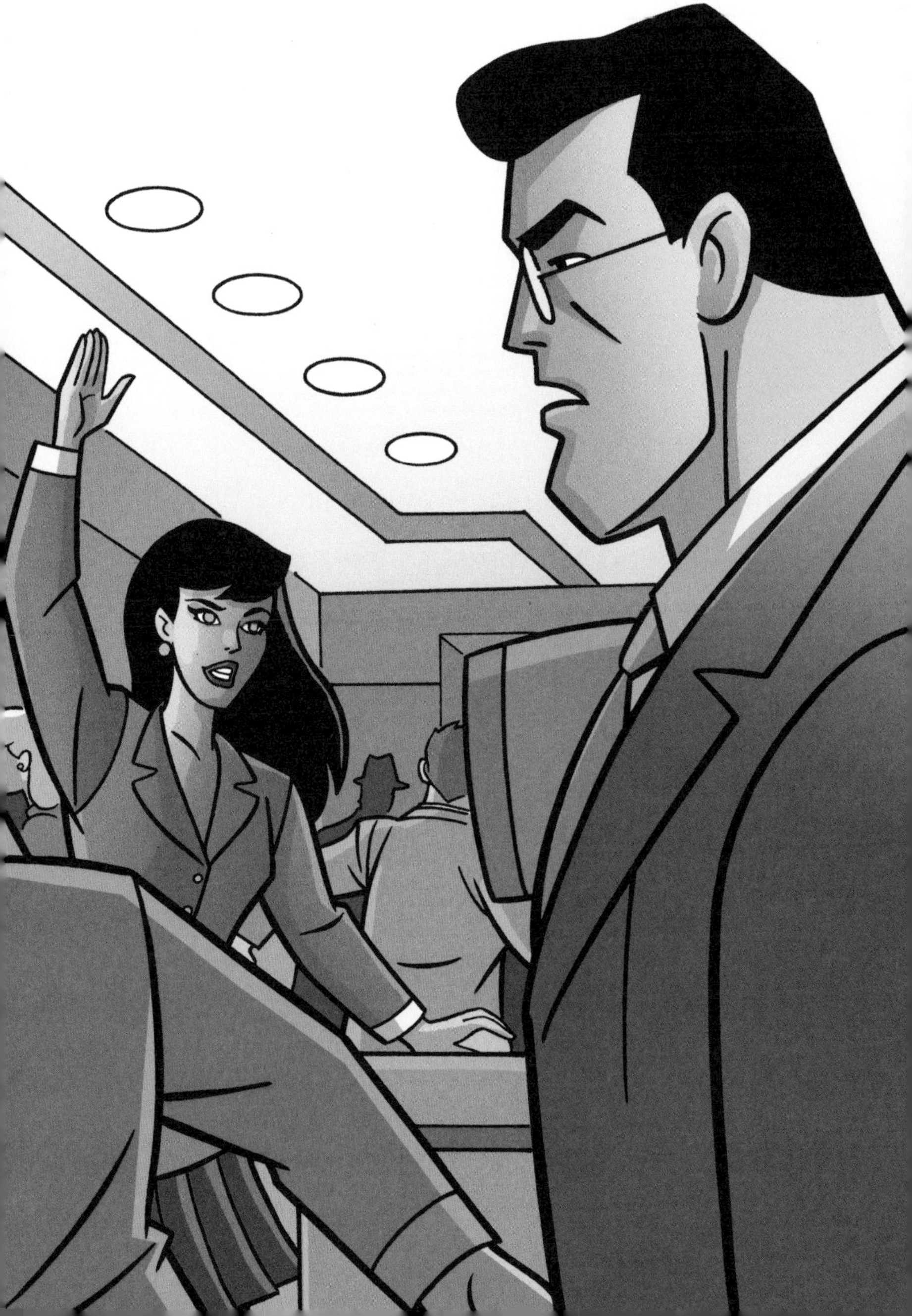

Clark turned to see the lovely but annoyed face of Lois Lane, the paper's smartest reporter.

"When Mala showed up this morning yelling at Superman, I went to cover them," Clark said. "And then —"

"Lane! Kent!" yelled the rough voice of their boss, *Daily Planet* editor Perry White. "Jax-Ur and Mala just showed up at City Hall. Find out what's going on!"

Lois and Clark ran to the newsroom's elevator. "Lois," Clark said carefully, "I was trying to report on Mala, but I kept hearing about weird disasters — streets getting torn up, mountains getting smashed, that sort of thing. And something happened to Superman. What's going on?"

"You didn't hear?" Lois asked.

Lois's voice turned dark. "Superman went crazy," she said.

They got out of the elevator and exited the Daily Planet building. Lois fished her cell phone out of her purse. She pulled up images from the news. "Look," she said.

On Lois's phone, Clark saw pictures of Jax-Ur disguised as Superman. In one picture, "Superman" dug Egypt's Nile riverbed into the shape of the five-pointed "S" symbol on Superman's costume. In another, he pushed the Greek islands into the shape of an "S." More pictures showed "Superman" carving the "S" symbol onto the face of Mount Everest.

Jax-Ur had reshaped Minnesota's lakes, Metropolis's streets, and Vermont's forests. "Superman" made them all to look like his "S" symbol.

Jax-Ur had even carved his own face into Mount Rushmore.

Clark tried to hide his growing anger at the things that Jax-Ur had done while disguised as Superman. "Did all of this stuff just happen this morning, Lois?" Clark asked.

"Of course it was this morning!" Lois snapped. "Where the heck have you been, Clark?"

That's why Mala led me on that chase, Clark thought. *She was getting me out of the way so Jax-Ur could dress up like me and do these awful things.*

"Every country Superman invaded tried to fight him," Lois said as they raced up the street to City Hall. "But they had no way to stop him."

Clark and Lois joined a crowd of people on the wide, marble courtyard outside City Hall. Jax-Ur and Mala floated in the air near the building's front doors. Clark saw that the dirt from their underground chase still covered them.

As Clark and Lois arrived, Mala glanced at them, but she didn't recognize Clark as Superman. *She doesn't know I have a secret identity,* Clark thought.

Jax-Ur recognized Lois and floated down to face her. Hundreds of cameras and microphones pointed at him. For a moment, he was silent.

Then Jax-Ur said, "I'm sorry, Ms. Lane."

"What do you mean?" Lois asked.

"When I first came to this world, I tried to conquer its people," Jax-Ur said.

"But you, young woman — you beat me. And you changed me," Jax-Ur explained. "I'm smart enough to learn from my mistakes. I shouldn't try to control humans. No one should. Not even Superman."

Jax-Ur slowly rose into the air. "I don't know why Superman is ripping up your world," he said. "But for the moment, I've stopped him."

Clark frowned as Jax-Ur spoke his lies. Jax-Ur ran his fingers down his filthy uniform. "As you can see, our battle with Superman has hurt both Mala and me," he said.

Both of you? Clark thought. Mala, he knew, had done most of the fighting and suffered most of the pain. For a moment, Clark thought he saw Mala glare angrily at Jax-Ur.

"Superman must come out of hiding sometime. Mala, scan the skies," Jax-Ur commanded.

At first, Mala didn't move. Clark thought she was going to refuse Jax-Ur's order. Reluctantly, Mala floated high into the air. She slowly looked up and down and side to side.

"We can't find Superman by ourselves," Jax-Ur went on. "I need the people of Earth to help us. After all, you know your world better than we do. And I promise: when I find him, I will capture him. And I will punish him!"

Some of the people around Clark cheered. But Lois, along with many others who knew Superman, was quiet. Clark wondered what the billions who had never met him were thinking.

With his super-hearing, Clark listened to the voices of people who were watching Jax-Ur on TV.

"Maybe Jax-Ur's not as bad as I thought," a housewife in London said. "Maybe he really has changed."

"I don't know what's happening with Superman, but someone has to stop him!" a baker in Cairo told his customers. "If Jax-Ur wants to try, then we should let him!"

"It takes a Kryptonian to stop a Kryptonian," said a mayor in Nigeria. "I hope he catches Superman fast!"

As Clark listened, he realized that Jax-Ur could hear the voices too. "I will repair the places that Superman attacked," Jax-Ur told the world. "We will work together — the people of Earth and me!"

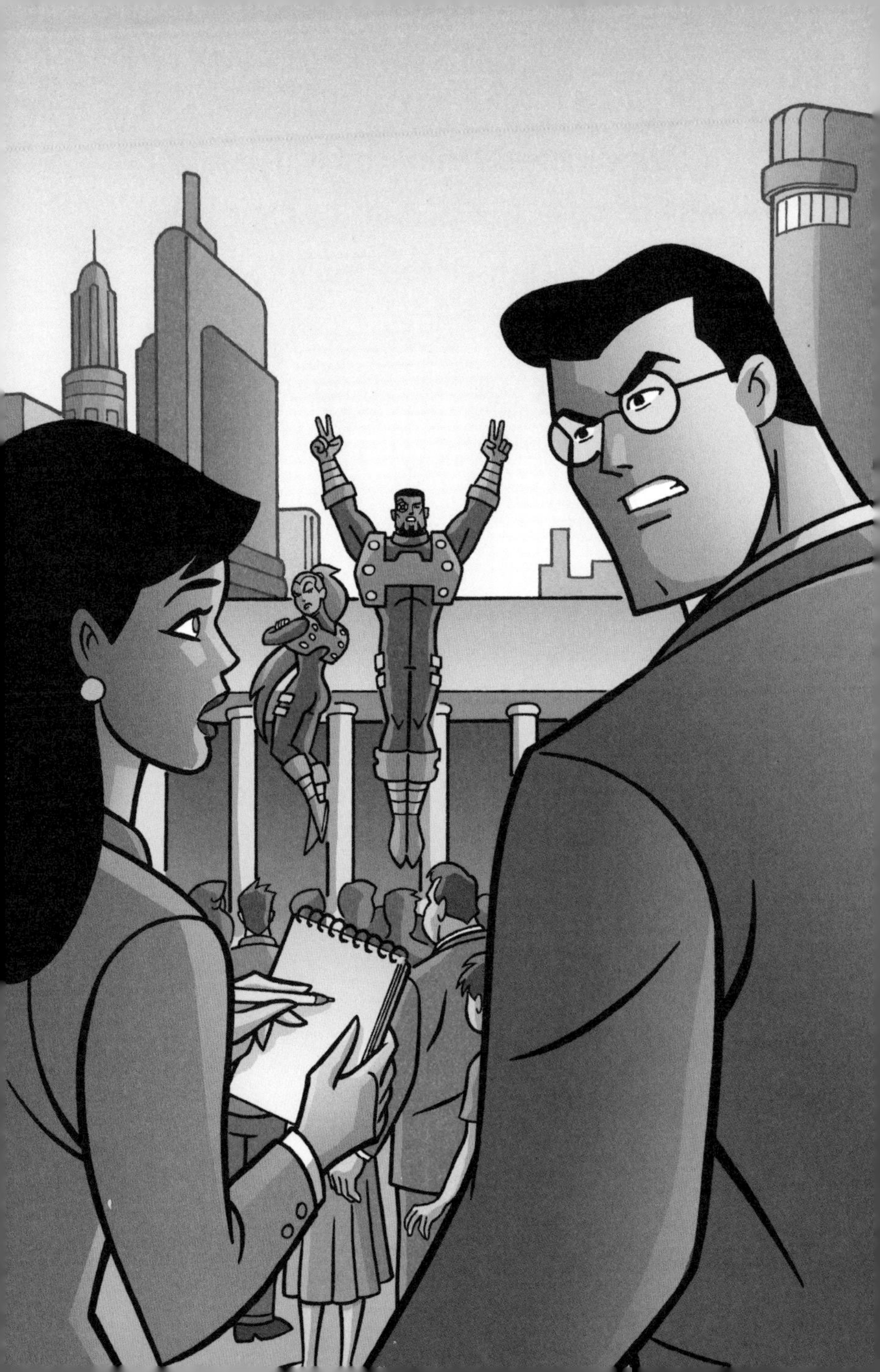

Clark watched Mala closely. For a brief moment, Mala frowned at Jax-Ur, but he was enjoying himself too much to notice. "If the people of Earth stand with me, I will help you make your world a paradise!" he shouted. "And no one, not even Superman, will stop us!"

The sun was high in the sky, but Clark felt cold. He could hear thousands of people cheering for Jax-Ur, but just as many people were silent. Clark could tell those silent ones didn't know what to think just yet. *I have faith in the people of Metropolis,* he thought. *But Jax-Ur is winning more supporters by the minute. I have to do something!*

CHAPTER 4

POPULARITY AND PAIN

"Clark, do you think people will believe Jax-Ur?" Lois asked. When she heard no response, she turned to look, but Clark was gone.

Clark had run into an alley next to City Hall. He kneeled down and glanced over his shoulder to make sure that no one could see him.

Clark lifted a manhole cover and slipped into the darkness below. He carefully slid the cover back into place and dropped into the greasy sewer. *SPLASH!*

He slipped his Clark Kent clothes off and shot away as Superman. He didn't like swimming through the sewer's gunk and slime, but its giant pipes had enough lead to block Jax-Ur and Mala from seeing him. He didn't want to fight the Kryptonians. He had a better plan in mind.

Superman emerged from the pipes into the open sea. He started digging beneath the ocean floor. For a moment, he looked up. He saw Jax-Ur and Mala crossing the sky at super-speed, hunting for him.

The Man of Steel kept digging. He had to move slowly and carefully. If he dug too hard and fast, he might trigger an earth tremor that could alert Jax-Ur and Mala to his location.

Far overhead, Jax-Ur and Mala sped up their search for Superman.

As minutes passed, Mala grew annoyed with their search. "We never should have let him slip away," she grumbled as they flew over Europe. "While you were making a speech to that crowd in Metropolis, we could have been hunting him."

"Be smart, Mala," Jax-Ur said. "That speech I gave will rally many people to our side. They will help us find Superman."

"Don't be so sure of yourself!" Mala snapped. "Listen."

Jax-Ur stretched his hearing to take in voices from all over the world. Now that his speech was over, the world's excitement was draining away.

On a talk radio station in Philadelphia, a man said, "Jax-Ur gave a nice speech, but I just can't trust him."

At the United Nations, a woman said, "Jax-Ur tried to take over the world once. He'll try to do it again." A religious leader in Jerusalem said, "Superman's been a good man. If something's changed him, we should help him." All over the world, people were doubting Jax-Ur.

"See?" Mala asked. "We need to find Superman fast! Otherwise, we'll lose the followers we need to take over this planet."

Jax-Ur frowned at Mala's bad news. Then he smiled. "I have an idea," he said. He turned and flew away. Mala sped after him.

While Jax-Ur and Mala were talking, Superman was digging. Soon, he arrived at the ice-covered Fortress of Solitude at the North Pole. Inside, he kept all kinds of strange things from other worlds.

Superman grabbed an alien item and wrapped it in his cape. Suddenly, he heard a voice shout, "News from Metropolis!"

The voice came from a computer. It tracked news reports of troubles that needed Superman's help. "Superman has just flown into town. He's smashing City Hall!" a TV reporter shouted.

Superman looked at the computer's screen. He saw Lois run to interview the fake Superman, not knowing it was Jax-Ur in disguise.

As Mala flew up behind him, the impostor reached for Lois. Instantly, the real Superman rocketed out of the Fortress.

Back in Metropolis, "Superman" lifted Lois off the ground by her arm. "What are you doing?" Mala asked.

"I'm drawing Superman out of hiding," Jax-Ur whispered back. "He'll never let me hurt this city — or this woman."

Jax-Ur looked over Mala's shoulder. He saw the real Superman flying toward them.

He dropped Lois to the ground. "Get out of my way!" the fake hero told Mala.

Mala said, "But you'll need my help!" **KA-POW!** Jax-Ur shoved the surprised Mala, sending her flying into the sky.

As Superman came near, Jax-Ur started to whip off his "Superman" disguise at super-speed. The world would see the real Superman attack Jax-Ur. They would think Superman had attacked Lois, and they'd call Jax-Ur a hero for saving her.

"No!" Superman shouted. He grabbed Jax-Ur halfway through his transformation.

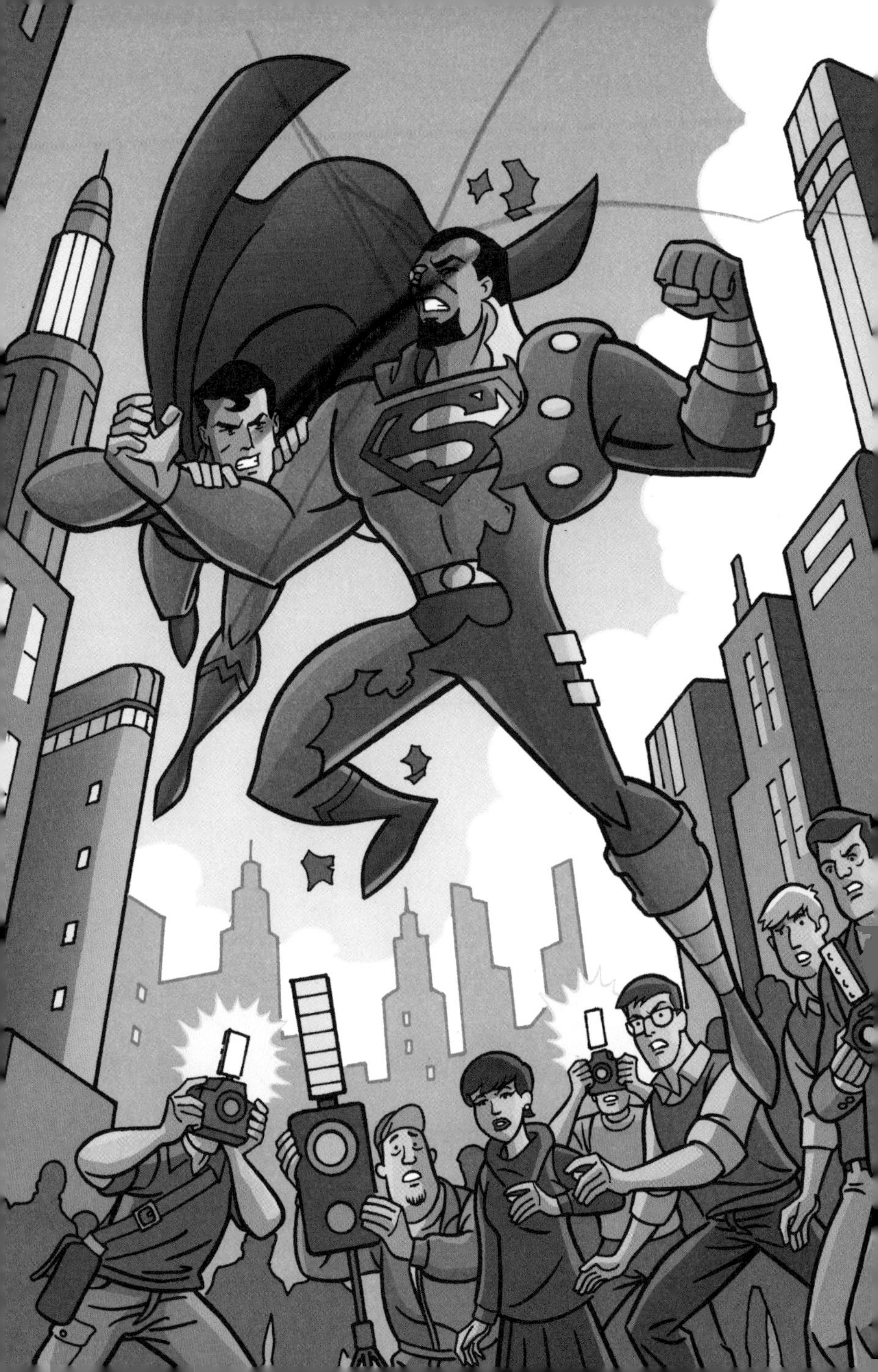

Superman held the exposed Jax-Ur in the air. "Now everyone can see who you really are!" he said.

People all over the world gasped when they saw that Jax-Ur had been wearing Superman's costume, pretending to be the Man of Steel.

Superman held Jax-Ur still with one powerful hand. With the other, he reached for the weapon wrapped in his cape.

Now it was Jax-Ur's turn to gasp. The weapon was the Phantom Zone projector. It was a computer box with a viewscreen, three dials, and a thick, powerful camera lens.

Superman aimed the Phantom Zone Projector at Jax-Ur. Just then, Mala slammed into Superman's back. WHAM!

Jax-Ur's shove had thrown Mala far away, but now she was back. And she was furious. As Superman crashed into one of the City Hall columns, he dropped the Phantom Zone Projector.

Mala lifted the stunned super hero up. She slammed him into the concrete over and over again. SLAM! SMASH! WHAM!

As Mala continued to smash Superman into the ground, Jax-Ur swiftly soared over to them and grabbed the Phantom Zone Projector. "Stop, Mala!" he said. Mala snarled in anger at Jax-Ur, but she did as she was told.

"Now hold him down!" Jax-Ur ordered. "It's time to end this once and for all."

Jax-Ur twisted the machine's dials. The projector hummed, charging to full power.

When the Phantom Zone Projector's lens glowed white, Jax-Ur knew it was fully charged and ready to fire.

Jax-Ur smiled. He aimed the lens at the Man of Steel.

"Good-bye forever, Superman!" he said.

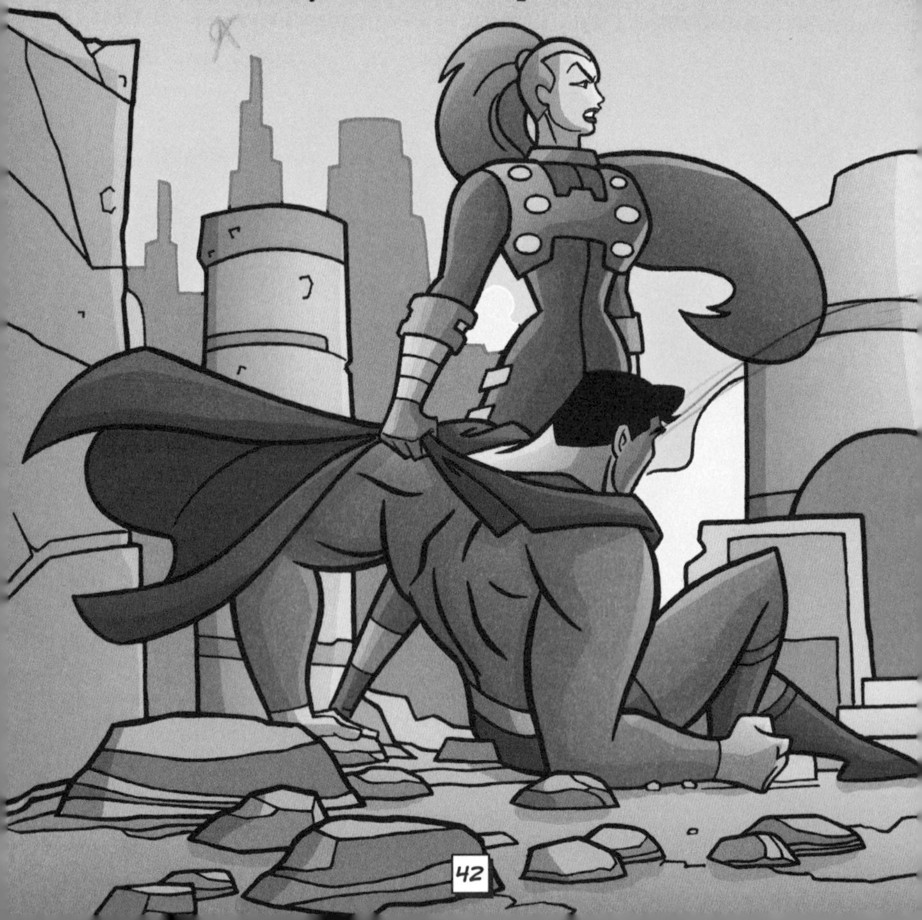

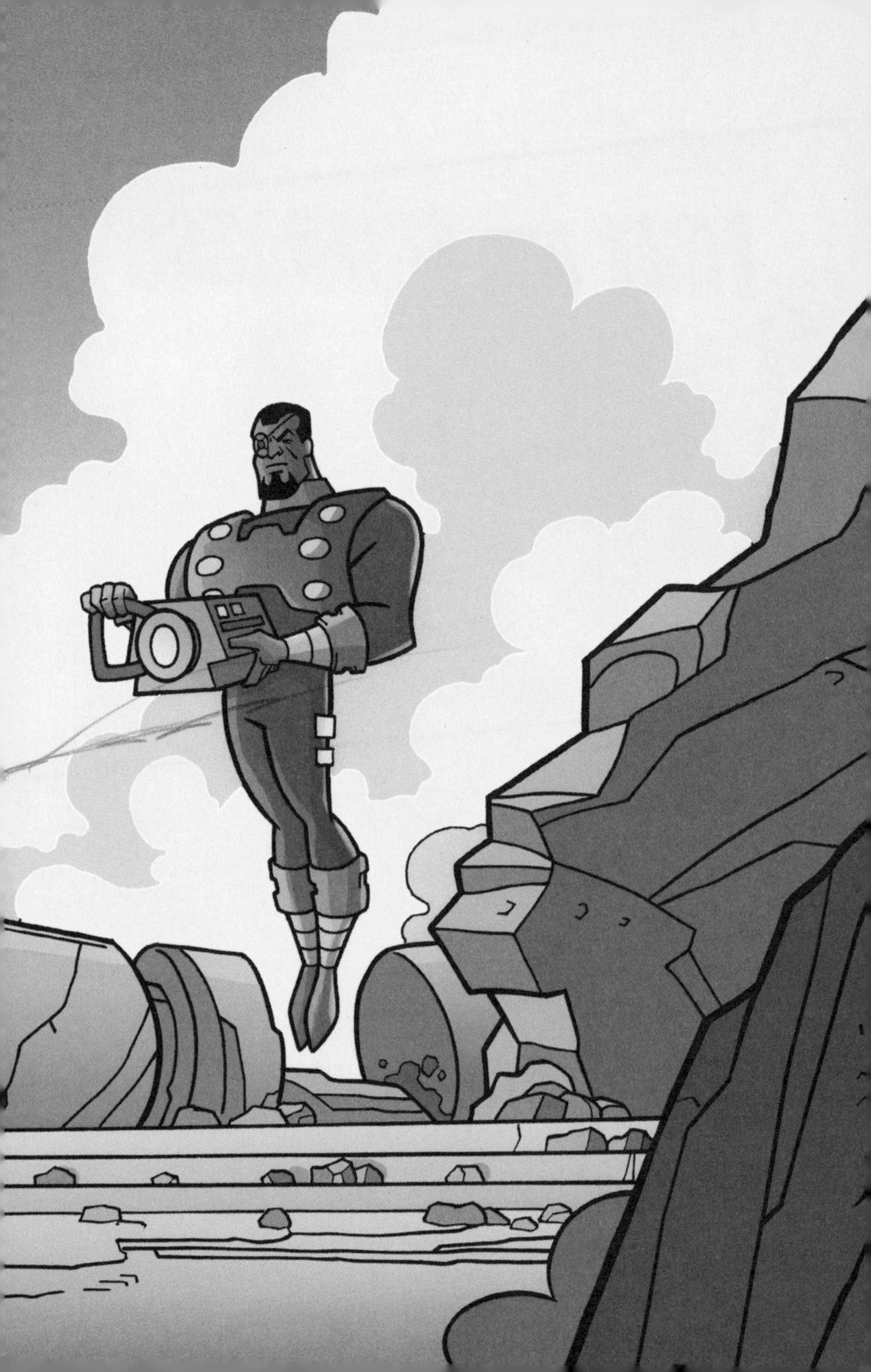

CHAPTER 5

FURY AND FRIENDSHIP

"Hold him still, Mala!" Jax-Ur demanded. "I can't get a good shot if you keep moving him around. And stay out of the way, or I'll send you to the Phantom Zone, too!"

"Quit giving me orders!" Mala yelled.

That's it! Superman thought. *I know how to beat them!*

Mala's nails dug into Superman's shoulders. Her frowning face was just inches from Superman's eyes.

"Jax-Ur gives you lots of orders, doesn't he?" Superman whispered into Mala's ear, but she didn't respond. "This whole plan was his idea, wasn't it? When you and I were fighting in space, and both of us were getting hurt, what was Jax-Ur doing? He was play-acting in a Superman costume! He had all the fun while you did all the hard work!"

Mala roared in fury. Superman pulled her closer. The Man of Steel smiled and said, "Mala, he's about to send you to the Phantom Zone!"

Mala looked over her shoulder at Jax-Ur. In that instant, Superman hurled himself at the big man. He yanked the Phantom Zone projector away from Jax-Ur.

At super-speed, Superman aimed and fired. 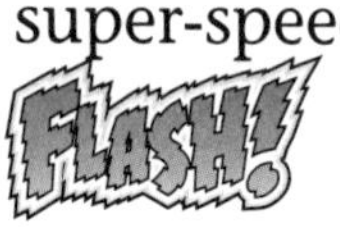
FLASH!

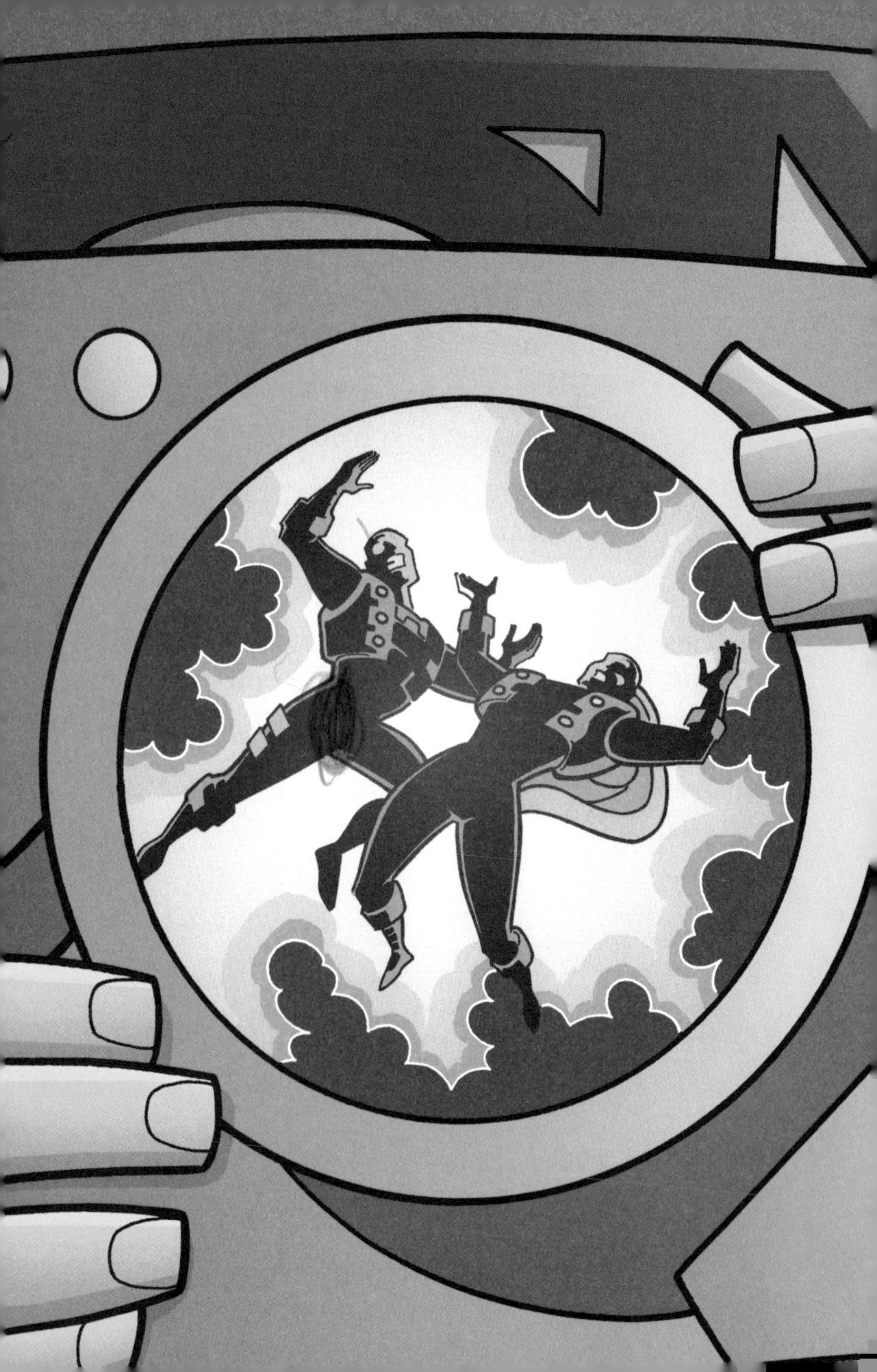

White light burst from the projector's lens and swallowed up Jax-Ur and Mala.

Superman looked into the projector's viewscreen. There floated Jax-Ur and Mala, screaming for help amid the Zone's dark and swirling clouds.

Superman hovered over the crowd of reporters nearby. They were quietly waiting for a word from their hero.

"Everything's all right," Superman told them. "Jax-Ur and Mala are trapped in the Phantom Zone." He looked around at City Hall's wrecked walls and floors. "As for me, I have some repairs to make."

Over the next few days, Superman fixed every mess that Jax-Ur had made. Wherever Superman went, people told him how sorry they were for ever doubting him.

When he finally finished repairing Metropolis, Clark was late for work. Clark nearly knocked Lois over as he sped back to his desk at the Daily Planet building. "Kent, sometimes I wish someone would disguise himself as *you* and take *your* place here," Lois grumbled.

Clark thought for a moment. "I don't know, Lois," he said. "I wouldn't want anyone pretending to be me."

"Honestly, Clark, do you think anyone would really *want* to be you?" Lois asked.

Clark smiled. "You never know, Lois. Maybe I live a secret life of adventure and excitement when I'm not at work!"

"Mild-mannered Clark Kent living a life of adventure and excitement?" Lois said, laughing. "Sure, Clark. Whatever you say."

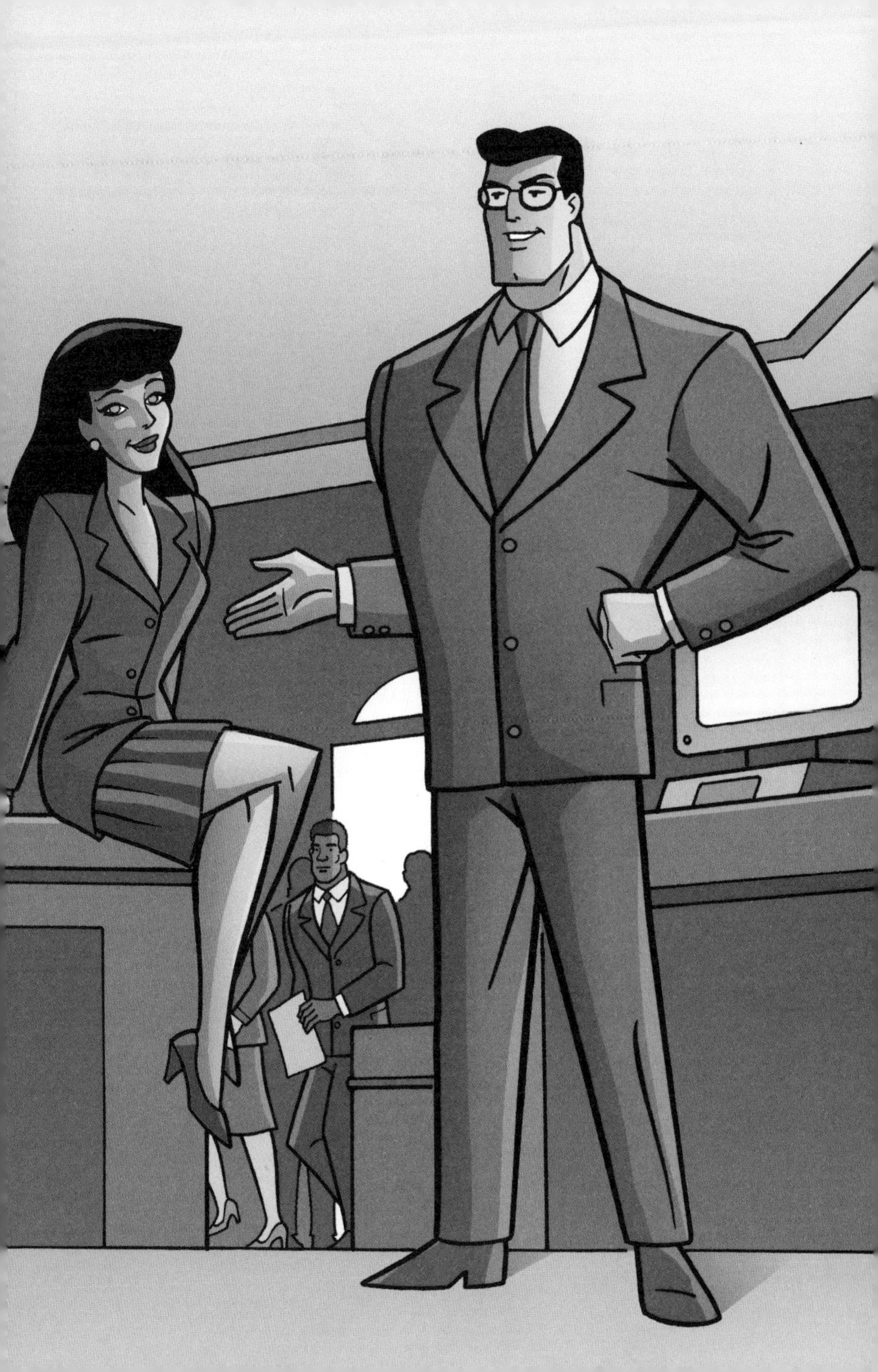

FROM THE DESK OF CLARK KENT

WHAT IS THE PHANTOM ZONE?

The Phantom Zone is an interdimensional world. It is used as a prison for only the most dangerous and violent criminals from Superman's home planet, Krypton. Anyone who enters the Zone's twisted void becomes trapped there, unable to interact with anything outside of it. The only way in or out is through the Phantom Zone Projector, a camera-like device that bridges this world and the Zone.

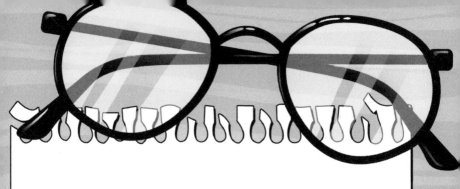

- The Phantom Zone Projector currently resides on Earth in Superman's secret base, the Fortress of Solitude. Because it can be used to free people from the Phantom Zone, Superman guards it closely. If the wrong person got their hands on it, untold evils would be released upon the world.

- The inhabitants of the Phantom Zone are considered to be neither dead nor alive, making it a very strange and confusing place. Many monsters and criminals are trapped there, making the Phantom Zone extremely dangerous, too.

- Superman once entered the Phantom Zone, and his physical body was twisted in knots. It took all of his strength and focus to pull himself together and escape.

- Because they exist outside of space and time, anyone trapped in the Phantom Zone does not age like a normal person would. Instead, when someone leaves the Zone, they will be the same age as when they first entered it.

BIOGRAPHIES

David Seidman is a comics writer, consultant, and publicist. He has written for Simpsons Comics, the nonfiction graphic novel *Samuel Morse and the Telegraph*, and the photo novel *Fantastic 4*. He was one of the founders of Disney Comics and has taught comic book writing at UCLA.

Erik Doescher is a freelance illustrator and video game designer based in Dallas, Texas. He attended the School of Visual Arts in New York City. Erik illustrated for a number of comic studios throughout the 1990s, and then moved to Texas to pursue videogame development and design. However, he has not completely given up on illustrating his favorite comic book characters.

Mike DeCarlo is a longtime contributor of comic art whose range extends from Batman and Iron Man to Bugs Bunny and Scooby-Doo. He resides in Connecticut with his wife and four children.

Lee Loughridge has been working in comics for more than 14 years. He currently lives in sunny California in a tent on the beach.

GLOSSARY

conquer (KONG-kur)—to defeat and take control of an enemy

coward (KOU-urd)—someone who is easily scared or runs away from a fearful situation

debris (duh-BREE)—the scattered pieces of something that has been broken or destroyed

disguised (diss-GIZED)—hid yourself by changing your appearance

emerged (i-MURJD)—came out into the open

furious (FYOO-ree-uhss)—extremely angry

impostor (im-POSS-tur)—someone who pretends to be something they are not

paradise (PAIR-uh-dise)—a place that is beautiful and peaceful

plunging (PLUHNJ-ing)—falling suddenly and sharply

reluctantly (ri-LUHK-tuhnt-lee)—if you act reluctantly, you hesitate to do something

DISCUSSION QUESTIONS

1. Who is more to blame for the damage done to Metropolis — Jax-Ur or Mala? Why?

2. If Superman didn't have superpowers, how else could he help to protect or improve the planet?

WRITING PROMPTS

1. Jax-Ur and Mala tried to trick the citizens of Metropolis. Have you ever been tricked? How did it make you feel? Have you ever tricked anyone? Write about it.

2. Clark Kent's secret identity is Superman. Why do you think he keeps his other identity a secret? What would happen if the world knew that mild-mannered reporter Clark Kent was also the Man of Steel?

3. Superman returns Jax-Ur and Mala to the Phantom Zone. Write another chapter to this book about their journey through the strange dimension. What does the Phantom Zone look like? Do they find their way out? You decide.

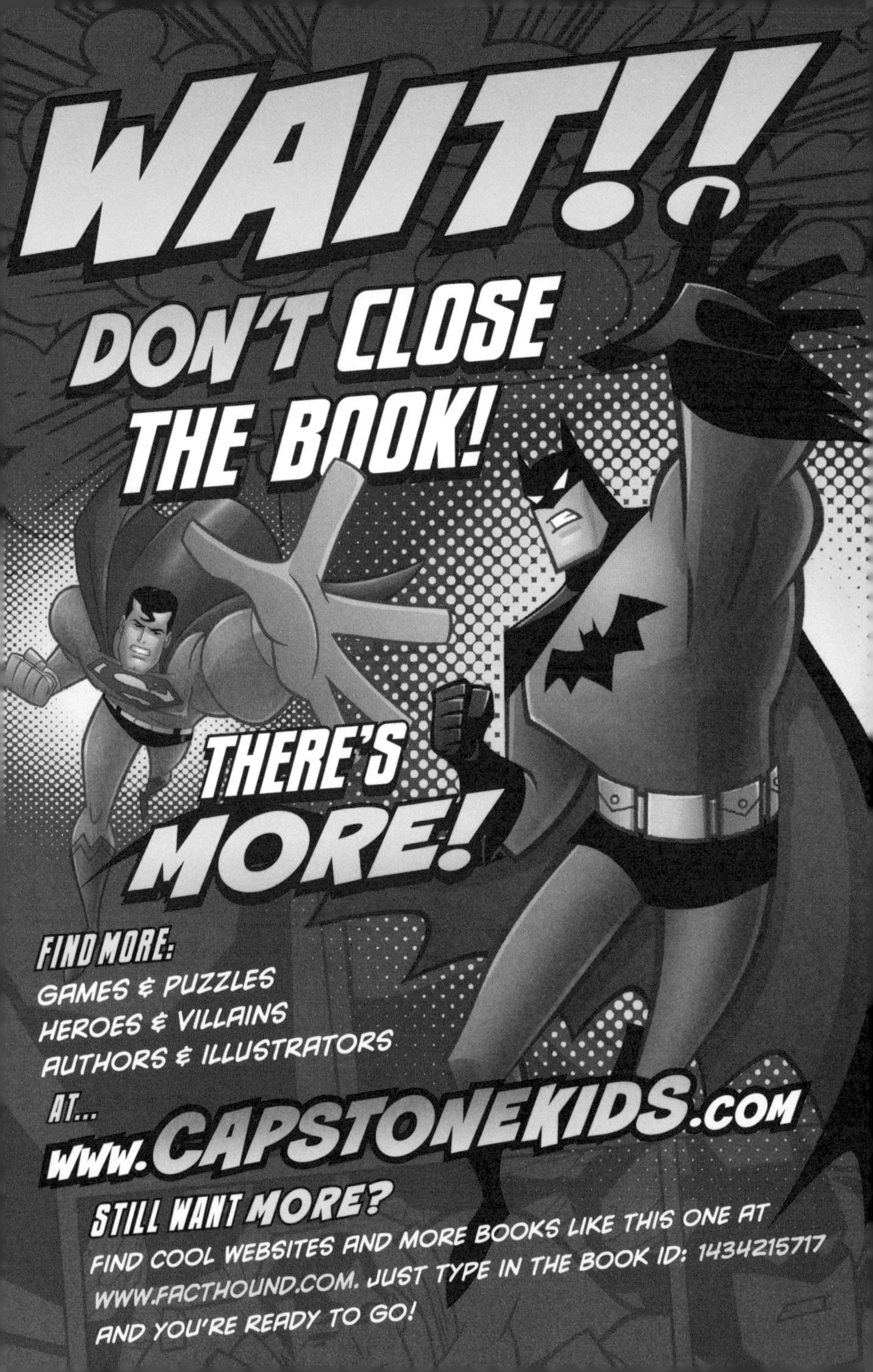

WAIT!!
DON'T CLOSE THE BOOK!
THERE'S MORE!
FIND MORE:
GAMES & PUZZLES
HEROES & VILLAINS
AUTHORS & ILLUSTRATORS
AT...
WWW.CAPSTONEKIDS.COM
STILL WANT MORE?
FIND COOL WEBSITES AND MORE BOOKS LIKE THIS ONE AT
WWW.FACTHOUND.COM. JUST TYPE IN THE BOOK ID: 1434215717
AND YOU'RE READY TO GO!

MORE NEW SUPERMAN ADVENTURES!

DEEP SPACE HIJACK

LITTLE GREEN MEN

PARASITE'S POWER DRAIN

LIVEWIRE!

THE KID WHO SAVED SUPERMAN

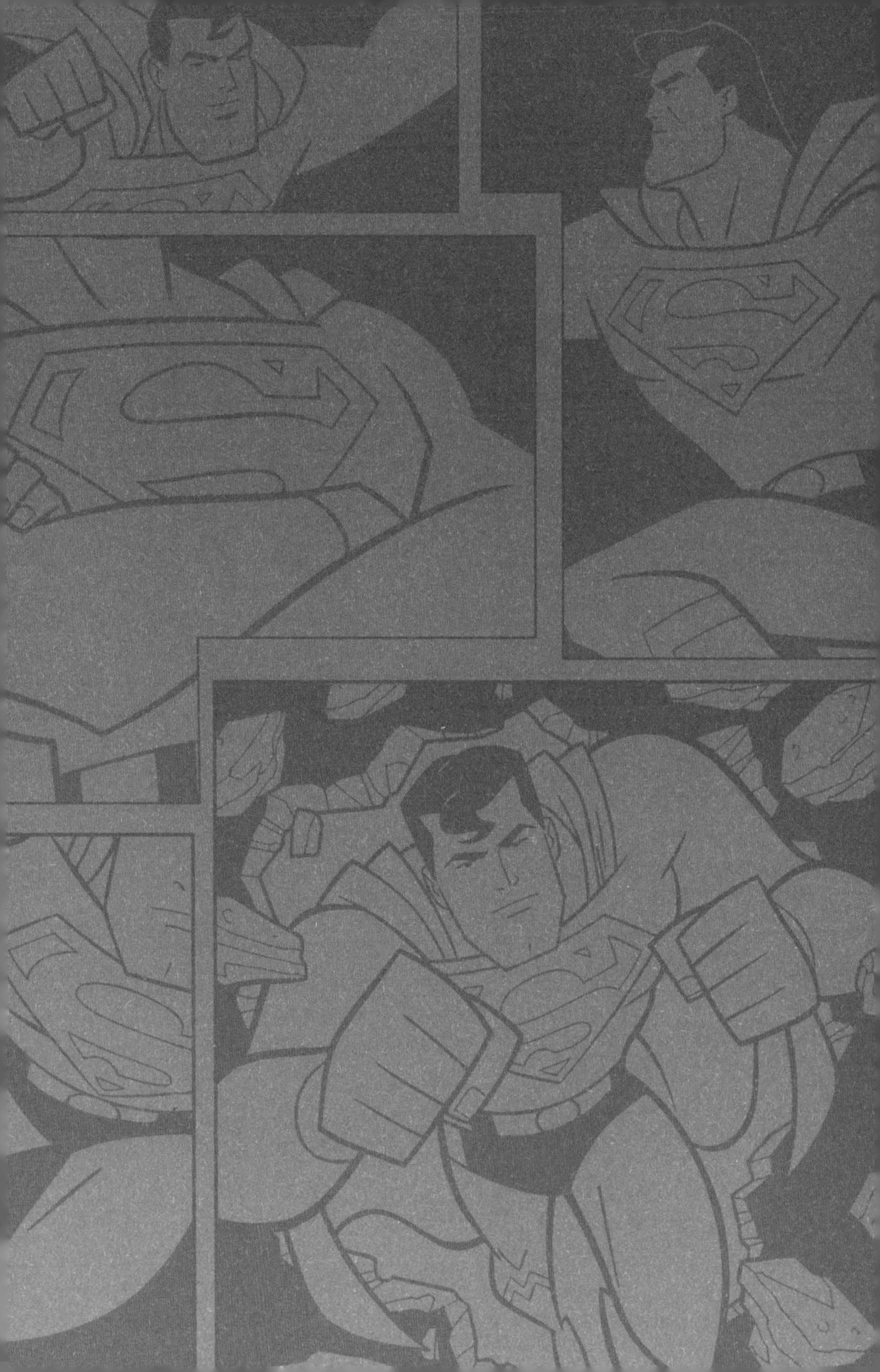

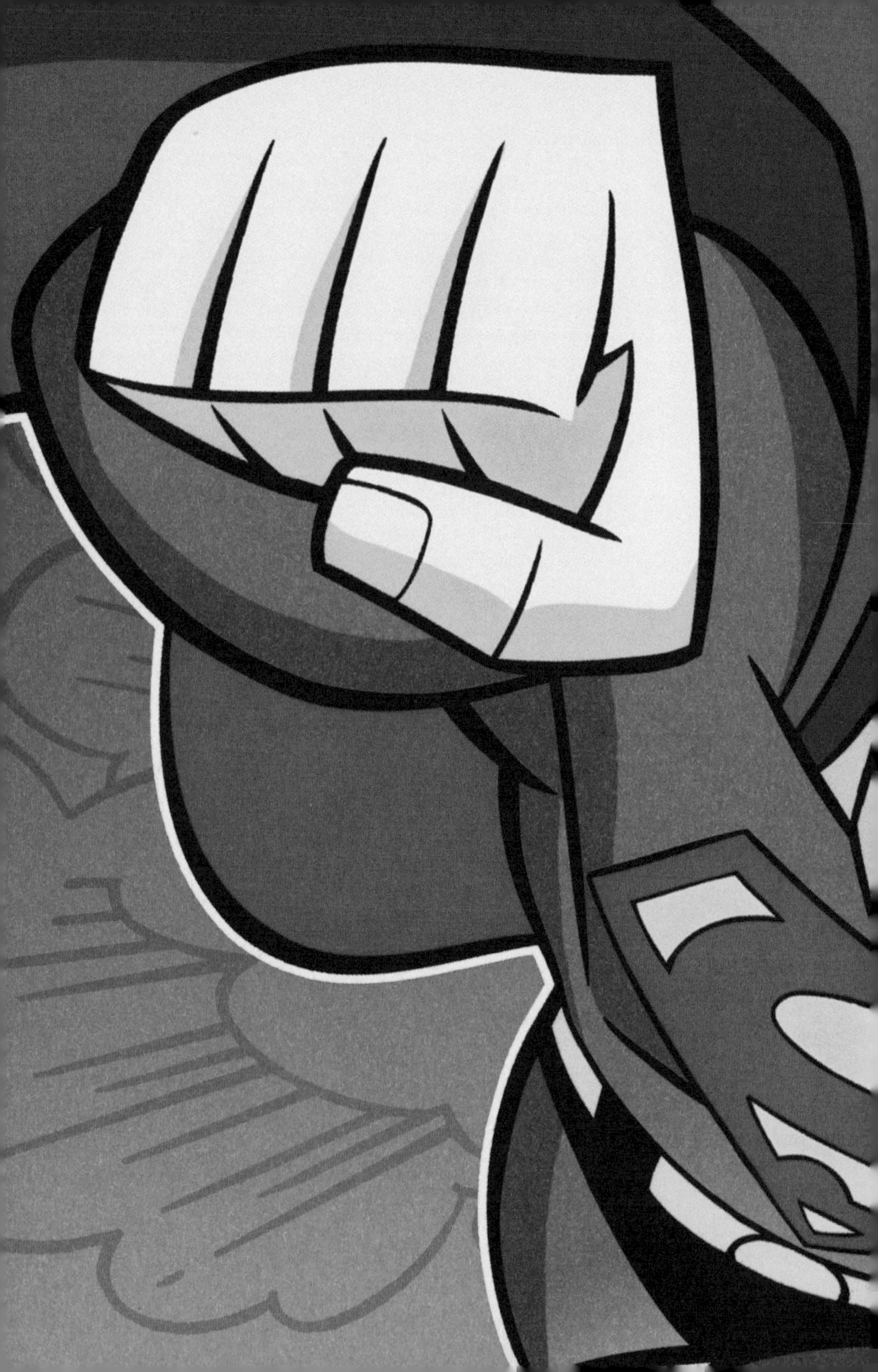

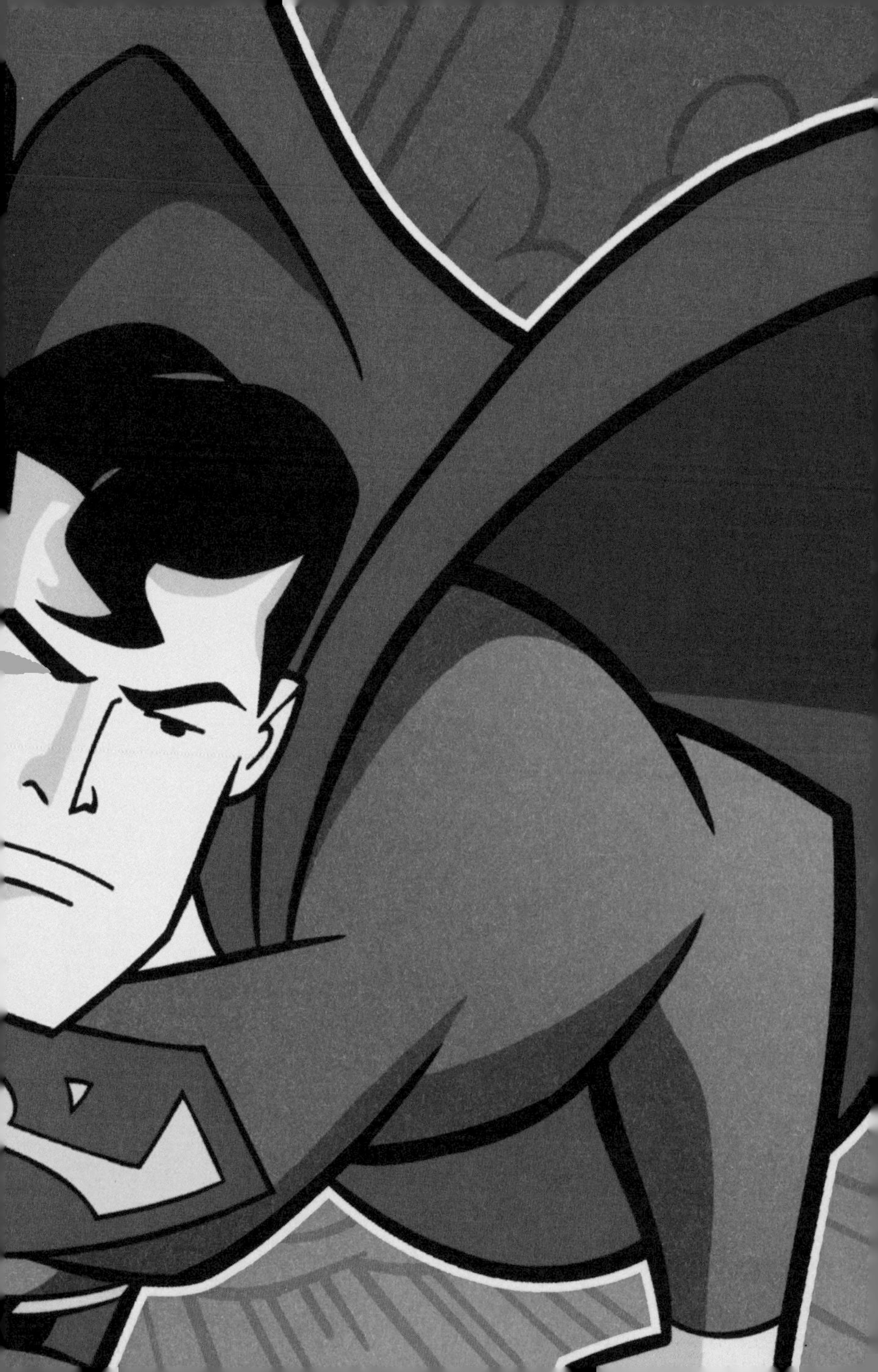